DOWN IN THE DUMPS

THE MYSTERY BOX

ALSO BY WES HARGIS:

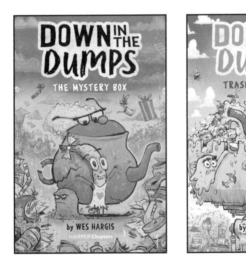

Read more Down in the Dumps books!

HARPER**Chapters**

DOWN IN THE DUMPS

THE MYSTERY BOX

WES HARGIS

HARPER

An Imprint of HarperCollins*Publishers*

For Clay

Down in the Dumps #1: The Mystery Box

Copyright © 2022 by HarperCollins Publishers

All rights reserved. Printed in the United States of America.

No part of this book may be used or reproduced in any manner whatsoever without
written permission except in the case of brief quotations embodied in critical articles
and reviews. For information address HarperCollins Children's Books, a division of
HarperCollins Publishers, 195 Broadway, New York, NY 10007.

www.harperchapters.com

Library of Congress Cataloging-in-Publication Data

Names: Hargis, Wes, author, illustrator.

Title: The mystery box / by Wes Hargis.

Description: First edition. | New York : Harper, [2022] | Series: Down in
the dumps ; #1 | Audience: Ages 6–10. | Audience: Grades 2–3. | Summary:
A rotten banana, a broken teapot, and a blob of goo living in the town
dump help a new arrival find his way home.

Identifiers: LCCN 2021030821 | ISBN 978-0-06-291010-3 (hardcover) |
ISBN 978-0-06-291012-7 (paperback)

Subjects: CYAC: Waste disposal sites—Fiction. | Refuse and refuse
disposal—Fiction. | Adventure and adventurers—Fiction.

Classification: LCC PZ7.1.H3678 My 2022 | DDC [Fic]—dc23

LC record available at https://lccn.loc.gov/2021030821

Typography by Torborg Davern

22 23 24 25 26   PC/LSCC   10 9 8 7 6 5 4 3 2 1

❖

First Edition

CONTENTS

It came like a wallop. Like an unexpected mule kick to the face.

It was a smell so bad it made your eyes water. It was like an onion sandwich wrapped in an old sock and stuffed in a dead moose. Only much, much WORSE.

GIT IN AND BRING THE CAT!

BWAWK!

Farmer Gunderson grabbed the cat, the dog, and all the chickens he could. He ran for the house.

The cause? It was the Westerfield Dump.

WESTERFIELD
WASTE TRANSFER
AND
RECYCLING
CENTER

A yellow-green stench drifted across the bridge.

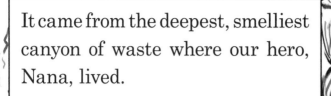

It came from the deepest, smelliest canyon of waste where our hero, Nana, lived.

Hello!

Nana was a dried-up banana. She had lived in the dump for as long as she could remember.

SIGH.
It's so lovely.

She lived at the dump with her two best friends, Ms. Kettle the teapot and Moreland the blob of goo.

Ms. Kettle likes things tidy!

GLO

Moreland was the WORST-smelling thing in the dump. He didn't talk much, and he didn't like hugs.

Ack!

cough!

But Nana often hugged him anyway.

You're just too CUTE!

TOOT!

The three friends lived in an old microwave stuck in the bottom of a canyon of trash in the far back corner of the dump.

Nana thought it was the coolest house ever.

She'd sometimes wonder how long things could remain so perfect.

It even beeps!

BEEP BEEP!

BLOP

1 2 3
4 5 6
7 0

START

First thing every morning, Nana started her day by going down to the conveyor belts to meet the new arrivals.

Nana would greet all the new trash as it arrived at The Great Pile.

C'mon, Moreland!

Welcome, Mr. TV! Right this way!

But this past Monday, Nana and Moreland arrived at The Great Pile and saw . . .

. . . a shiny red box shoot off the belt!

Nana and Moreland followed the voice.

There in the pile they found one of the strangest things Nana had ever seen—a talking box! One that didn't have a bit of goop, dirt, or even sludge on it.

And the box said:

TED-TABULOUS!

And then it said:

TED-TACULAR!

They both jumped back.

Egads!

PLINK, PLINK!

15

We have to bring this thing back home.
Let's use this old rusty roller skate!
But before they could leave, the Mungle Brothers showed up.
You read two chapters. That's over 400 words!
1
2

CHAPTER 3
DOWN, DOWN, DOWN

The Mungle Brothers were the meanest and dirtiest roaches ever to creep around the dump.

Just grrreat.

TED-CREDIBLE!

The box scared the Mungles away. Then Moreland poofed out into a giant snot bubble, scaring them further.

Nice work!

Nana was too busy yelling and Moreland was too busy deflating himself to notice that the box had begun to roll away.

Nana and Moreland dashed after the box as it bumbled and bounced down the trail.

Fast as they ran, neither of them was fast enough!

The box shot over the lip of the canyon, right toward their home.

As the dust cleared, they saw that the box had broken open. There sat a big, brown, fluffy new teddy bear.

Gasp!
Oh my stars!
It's a BEAR!

He was the cleanest thing they had ever seen.

Nana and Moreland introduced themselves. Then Nana introduced Ms. Kettle.

Welcome to the dump.

Hi, I'm Teddy Tedd Ted. Nice to meet you all.

And sorry to ask, but what's a dump?

Just then, a loose pizza box spun down and hit Ted on the head.

BONK

Ted let out a jingle as he fell to the ground.

Heavens to Betsy! I remember that tune!

Ms. Kettle ran and pulled out a giant catalog. She set it in front of the old microwave.

Ms. Kettle gave Teddy Tedd Ted an ice pack. He began to feel better. Sort of.

Where's little Reginald P.?

I'm his special gift, you know.

He's lost it.

29

Nana, Moreland, and Ms. Kettle knew what they had to do. They had to get this bear back home. But how?

Well, we can't go past the crows.

Or the slime pits.

I like the slime pits.

And we definitely can't go past the Dozer of DOOM.

In the distance, the Dozer rose as if it heard its name called.

We have to get to The Great Gate.

Together, they climbed up an old fridge with a broken door. It had some squishy old pickles inside.

Peering across the dump, out into the world beyond, they saw the scary journey ahead.

Oh my biscuits! It's so far!

What choice do we have?

We have to get Teddy home.

Okay, team!

Let's pack!

Moreland liked peanuts, so he stuck a few into his clear, pinkish-green goo. Ms. Kettle bustled about gathering supplies. Nana paused as she realized . . .

I've never gone so far from home before, Moreland.

I'm scared.

1 2 3 4

Ready to set out on their journey, Nana, Moreland, Ms. Kettle, and Ted gathered at the base of The Great Pile.

I've written a few words for our voyage.

Oh, how exciting!

But just as Nana was about to give her speech, a giant machine shook the ground as it moved toward them. Scared, they ran toward the only safe place they could see.

THIS WAY!

Inside the cave, the air was thick and musty. This place stank, but it was a different kind of stink. It was the stench of OLD trash.

The peanuts Moreland ate
were making him glow green.

Ms. Kettle held Moreland up like a lamp, and the four friends headed deeper into the cave.

Lead us out of here, Moreland!

The cave opened up to a lake so big they couldn't see the other side.

I'm afraid we have to cross this.

But then, out of nowhere, a soft jingle started echoing around them.

That one wasn't me. I swear.

The jingling got loud until it turned into a song.

The ladies all say that my boots look fine cuz I polish them up with my Buffalo Shine!

Paddling toward them was an antique shoe polish tin using a soggy cotton swab as an oar.

Ms. Kettle thought quickly. She floated out to the tin with a bit of Nana's plastic bag dress to patch his hole.

Hold still, dear!

Ms. Kettle, you can float!

Good as new!

Turned out, Ms. Kettle was the perfect boat! Moreland got on her spout, Ted sat on her lid, and Nana went on her handle.

Tallyho!

They drifted off as Mr. Tin waved goodbye with his squishy swab.

Good to meet you, Mr. Tin.

We really must get Ted to the gate.

They floated away into the gloopy sea of stench and bubbles.

Be careful! Watch out for the Dozer of Doom!

The floating, huddling group bobbed along for a while on the greenish slime.

I feel a breeze.

I wish Ms. Kettle had a sail.

Which gives me an idea.

Nana whispered to Moreland.

PSST
PSST
PSST

THOOMP!

He's a slime sail!

Ms. Kettle had packed a lunch for everyone. She made gooberry tarts with curdled milk. Even Ted liked the oozing treat.

Yum! I'm new to food . . . I'm new to everything, I guess.

Moreland yawned a big sleepy yawn, and then everyone was yawning.

YAWN YAWWWN YAWWN

ZZZZ ZZZZ ZZZZ ZZZZZ

It wasn't long before they all fell asleep. Nana started to dream.

Nana dreamed that Ms. Kettle-ship was flying . . .

. . . over The Great Pile . . .

. . . over the conveyor belt.

. . . and over the head of the Dozer of Doom.

1 2 3 4 5

CHAPTER 6
SHLORP!

Nana, Moreland, Ms. Kettle, and Ted woke up to quite a surprise.

They tried popping the bubbles. Then suddenly, the bubbles parted, and the four friends began falling down a raging river of slime.

The river flowed into a round room and then spun toward a giant whirlpool.

53

They were sucked into a network of pipes deep under The Great Pile.

54

Then almost as quickly as they were sucked in—

THOOOMP!

—they shot out into a river of bright blue slime before washing up on a warm sand trash shore.

Suddenly, a giant screeching sound shook the ground around them.

My lid's rattling!

So are my teeth!

57

They ran away from the great beast and climbed to the top of the bank overlooking a huge open area.

Something is eerie about all this.

Yeah, where's all the trash?

CHAPTER 7
BIRD BARF

They saw they were STANDING on flattened trash.

Thanks for the lovely offer.

But we'd rather not be flattened.

We've got places to go!

The three friends turned to leave when across the horizon—

Crows!

60

The friends ran as fast as they could until they came to a rusty metal fence.

Why are we so afraid of crows?

NANA!

Okay, I get it now.

61

But then More-
land rolled in to
the rescue.

The crow dropped Nana
and—

SNAP!

MORELAND!

GULP!

But then . . .

GLURP

GURGLE

GORGL.

62

BLARGF!

The bird moaned weakly and flew away.

Moreland rolled upright and shook himself off.

HACK!

I hate when that happens.

You saved me, Stinky!

63

Nana, Ted, and Moreland climbed inside Ms. Kettle's teapot.

This way.

Nana, Ted, and Moreland stayed hidden while Ms. Kettle followed the strange little can opener to see—

Big Bettie.

Wow, it's beautiful!

But after she thanked the strange little can opener and turned to leave, Ms. Kettle tripped and lost her balance.

69

CHAPTER 8
THE DOZER OF DOOM

The Dozer of Doom towered over them.

Ted fainted. Moreland turned into a snot bubble. Ms. Kettle gasped. But Nana, she simply stood there. She had noticed something surprising.

Urp!

Nana tried to seem brave. After all, it wasn't every day that she talked to scary giant machines.

She leaned back and tooted her rusty silver whistle.

Just then, a big red garbage truck pulled up. A door opened and a man in dusty work boots hopped out.

76

As the conveyor belt took Nana, Ms. Kettle, and Moreland back to their home, they waved goodbye to Ted.

Nana, Ms. Kettle, and Moreland zoomed off above the mountains of garbage all the way back to the old microwave.

Nana thought about what they had done for Ted, and her mushy banana heart felt warm.

They shot off the belt at the end of the line.

The Mungles greeted them—with spitballs.

Being back home after their big adventure, Nana noticed that everything was stickier and stinkier than she remembered.

TART

SIGH

She hadn't thought it was possible, but she loved her home even more.

But she couldn't help but wonder what would happen to Ted.

CHAPTER 9
WHERE'S TED?

As it turned out, Ted wound up in the snuggly arms of a little girl named Chloe. Every day, they would have tea, go on walks, and eat cake.

I knew I'd like cake!

Ted would also tell her stories of his grand adventures across the dump. When he got to the scary parts, he'd still jingle.

Just a little bit!

From time to time, Ted would write Nana, Ms. Kettle, and Moreland to tell them about his new life.

But Ted didn't know where to mail his letters.

Until he realized . . .

. . . all he had to do was throw his letters in the trash.

And sure enough, Nana, Ms. Kettle, and Moreland got every last one.

CONGRATULATIONS!

You've read **9** chapters,

87 pages,

and **2,541** words!

All your help paid off!

SUPER STINKY GAMES

THINK

Nana loves the Westerfield Dump. Last week, Nana met 357 new pieces of trash when they came down the conveyor belt. If the same number of new pieces of trash arrived at the dump every day, how many new friends did Nana meet each day?

FEEL

At the end of the story, Teddy Tedd Ted writes a letter to his friends back at the dump. Do you have a friend who moved away or a relative who doesn't live nearby? Write them a letter and tell them about the last fun thing you did.

ACT

Teddy Tedd Ted found a new home with a little girl who loves him. Do you have a favorite stuffed animal or toy? Draw a picture of it.

WES HARGIS is an author-illustrator living in the desert of Arizona. He began his career in the Tucson newspaper industry and honed his craft late at night while landscaping in the hot sun during the day. The first children's book he ever illustrated was *Jackson and Bud's Bumpy Ride*. Since then, Wes has worked on lots of books, including *When I Grow Up* (a *New York Times* bestseller!) by "Weird Al" Yankovic and the Let's Investigate with Nate science series by Nate Ball.

Wes likes to draw on scratchy paper, but these days he mostly uses a big tablet. Wes loves hanging out with his kids and exploring the desert. He also loves making his own Mexican food and the color yellow-green (like Moreland).

He's married to his lovely wife, Debbie. They have three opinionated kids, two evil cats, and one happily clueless dog. And plants. Lots of plants.